DISNEP

Anna & Elsa

Memory and Magic

For Quinn —E.D.

Copyright © 2015 Disney Enterprises, Inc. All rights reserved. Published in the
United States by Random House Children's Books, a division of Random House
LLC, 1745 Broadway, New York, NY 10019, and in Canada by Random House
of Canada Limited, Toronto, Penguin Random House Companies, in conjunction
with Disney Enterprises, Inc. Random House and the colophon are registered
trademarks of Random House LLC.

randomhousekids.com

ISBN 978-0-7364-3285-6 (hardcover) — ISBN 978-0-7364-8217-2 (lib. bdg.)

Printed in the United States of America
10 9 8 7 6 5 4 3 2 1

Disney

Anna & Elsa

Memory and Magic

By Erica David
Illustrated by Bill Robinson

Random House  New York

Chapter 1

"One, two, three!" Princess Anna of Arendelle shouted. Her feet were perched at the edge of a floating slab of ice. The ice floe bobbed through the rapids of Odin's Fjord, an icy waterway. The narrow lane of water had steep banks made of stone. At the count of three, Anna leaped from one patch of ice to another.

"Anna, be careful!" Elsa called from the royal barge. But there was no stopping her younger sister. Even though Elsa was queen and ruled the village, there were times when it seemed that Anna was really the one in charge. She had been out of the boat and on the ice before anyone had the chance to try to talk her out of it.

"Careful is my middle name!" Anna replied.

"Really?" Elsa asked doubtfully. "The last time I checked, it was Not Nearly Careful Enough!"

Anna skipped back and forth across the floating sheets of ice. When she landed on an ice floe next to the royal barge, she hopped on board, joining her sister.

"You know that I could use magic to help you?" Elsa asked her. "I could freeze the water under your feet."

"It's more fun this way!" Anna insisted.

The barge they stood on was a long, slow-moving boat. *Too slow,* Anna thought. Normally, it was used to transport goods to neighboring villages. Today, Elsa had suggested they take it on a tour of the fjords.

Anna had been enjoying the tour, but she thought it could use a little more action. When she saw the swirling rapids, she knew it was the perfect place to try ice hopping. And she was right. She loved the thrill of jumping from one sheet of ice to the next. The bubbling currents of the fjord made for an exciting challenge.

"Your turn!" Anna said to Elsa.

Elsa gazed out at the choppy waves. "I don't know, Anna . . . ," she said hesitantly. "It looks fun, but I think I'll pass."

"You'll be fine," Anna told her. "Besides, we made a deal. I try something you like, you try something I like."

"Are you sure this is what you like?" asked Elsa. She watched the ice floes bob and dip on the current.

"Positive," Anna said. "And no magic!"

Elsa squared her shoulders and took a deep breath. She got ready to take the plunge. Actually, the point was *not* to plunge. The point was to land safely on the ice. Elsa jumped off the deck.

"Your Majesty!" the boat captain cried in alarm.

"It's okay, Klaus," Anna said. "She meant to do that."

Elsa landed easily on a patch of ice. She looked unsure, but she was safe and sound. She found her balance as the ice floated on the choppy water. After a moment, she hopped to the next sheet of ice drifting downstream.

Elsa leaped from floe to floe for a few moments and quickly returned to the barge. As she climbed on deck, Anna congratulated her.

"Not bad for your first time ice hopping," she said.

"I think it'll be my last," Elsa replied.

"You didn't like it?" Anna asked.

"It's definitely exciting," Elsa answered. "But maybe a little *too* thrilling for my taste."

Anna snorted at the word "taste." The day before, it had been Anna's turn to try something Elsa liked. Elsa had decided she wanted her sister to eat pickled herring, her favorite fish. Anna had hated the smell of it as a child, so she never ate it. Elsa thought it was high time for Anna to give it another try.

When the castle chef had set the large platter of fish in front of Anna that day, she'd wrinkled her nose. *Pickled herring*

has a funny smell, she thought. The scent drifted through the dining room. Anna's stomach lurched.

Reluctantly, she placed a tiny piece of fish on her plate. Elsa had already started eating. She'd been looking forward to the meal all day. She gazed at Anna expectantly.

Anna speared a forkful of fish and brought it to her lips. The trouble was she didn't want to open her mouth.

"Don't be so dramatic," Elsa said. "The worst that could happen is that you don't like it."

"I'm not so sure. What if this fish pickles my insides?" Anna joked.

Elsa smiled patiently.

Slowly, Anna opened her mouth. She

tucked the fish inside and squeezed her lips shut. She chewed quickly. The faster she chewed it, the less time she had to taste it. Finally, Anna managed to swallow it down.

"So, what do you think?" Elsa asked.

"It's just as weird as I thought it would be," Anna said.

"Weird? Pickled herring is the cook's specialty!" said Elsa.

Anna shrugged. "Sorry," she said. "But I *especially* don't like it." She wrinkled her nose again. "How can you eat this stuff?"

Elsa didn't reply. She simply shoveled another forkful into her mouth. She smiled with pleasure as she gobbled it

down. Judging by the look on her face, one would think pickled herring was the most delicious food in the world. It was clear that Anna and her sister had very different tastes.

*

Back on the boat, Anna was surprised that Elsa didn't love ice hopping as much as she did. It was so much better than eating pickled fish.

"Instead of trying things only one of us likes, let's find something we both like to do," Anna said.

"I have the perfect idea," Elsa told her.

That night, the sky over Arendelle was

filled with stars. The Northern Lights shimmered in the distance. They were so bright they lit up the entire village.

Anna and Elsa were sitting comfortably in the back of a beautiful sleigh. The royal coachman was taking them for a ride under the stars.

"This was a wonderful idea," Anna said.

"I thought you'd like it," Elsa replied. "There's no pickled herring in sight."

Anna laughed. She glanced at Elsa. These past few weeks, they had been spending more and more time together. They had gone ice fishing with Kristoff and paid a visit to Oaken's sauna.

Anna realized that it didn't matter what kind of adventure they had. As long as she and Elsa were together, they had fun. It had been that way even when they were little girls. In Anna's earliest memories, she and Elsa played together all the time.

Anna felt happy when she thought of those childhood days. But when she tried to recall specific things, she only remembered laughter and snow. In the sleigh under the beautiful winter sky, Anna furrowed her brow. There had to be more than just laughter and snow. She was sure of it.

"What's wrong?" Elsa asked, noticing her sister's expression.

"Nothing," Anna said. "Remember how we used to play together as girls?"

"Yes," Elsa replied, smiling.

Anna chewed her lower lip. There was something nagging at her.

"Well, I'm not sure I do," she said uneasily.

Chapter 2

The next morning, Anna tried to shake off the strange feeling from the night before. She'd only been tired, she told herself. She had so many memories of good times with Elsa, it was hard to keep track. That was all. She was sure the details would come back to her.

Anna and Elsa took a walk in the woods with Kristoff, Sven the reindeer, and Olaf the snowman. It was the perfect winter morning—crisp, cold, and made for a snowball fight. Anna grabbed a handful of fresh snow and made a ball. She lobbed it at Kristoff, who pulled a face like he was angry, then smiled. He chased Anna through the trees and pelted her with snowballs.

Olaf ran straight for Elsa. He hurled himself at her knees. The snowman playfully tried to knock her over.

"Olaf! No tackling. This is a snowball fight!" Elsa exclaimed. "You're supposed to throw snowballs!"

"But I *am* snowballs! I'm made of snow!" Olaf explained cheerfully. "I just threw myself!"

Elsa laughed and climbed to her feet. She dusted the snow from her skirts. "I think that's an unfair advantage," she said.

"Oh. I never thought of that," Olaf said. "Truce?"

"Truce," Elsa agreed.

"How about a warm hug to seal the deal?" Olaf suggested. Olaf loved warm hugs.

"Sure," Elsa replied. She leaned down and hugged the little snowman. Olaf was delighted.

With Kristoff on her heels, Anna ran back to the clearing and saw Elsa and Olaf hugging. Something about the situation tugged at her memory. Olaf asked for warm hugs all the time, but that wasn't it. She tried to remember building a snowman

with Elsa when they were younger. They
must have built snowmen together. But
Anna couldn't remember exactly. The
more she tried to recall, the more confused
she became. All she could remember was
snow and laughter.

"Elsa, we've built snowmen together,
haven't we?" Anna asked.

"Of course," Elsa replied.

"It's funny. I can't seem to remember," said Anna.

Elsa grew quiet. "I'm sure you will soon," she said.

"It's kind of weird, though," Anna said, scratching her head. "Why would I forget something like that?"

"Maybe you're getting old," Olaf said brightly.

"I'm not getting old!" Anna exclaimed.

Elsa looked away. Anna had the strangest feeling that her sister knew something about her memory problem. For some reason, Elsa didn't want to tell her what she was thinking.

Kristoff was standing beside Anna,

petting Sven. Sven looked from Elsa to Anna and back again with a worried expression. Kristoff pretended to speak for Sven in a silly voice.

"'Gee, Kristoff. Why is everyone standing around awkwardly talking when there's a snowball fight going on?'

"I don't know, Sven," Kristoff replied in his normal voice. "Maybe they're scared to lose!"

Kristoff resumed the fight, hurling snowballs at Anna and Elsa. Both sisters ducked and ran for cover. Anna forgot her worries as she dodged the flying snow.

But once Elsa was safely behind a tree, she didn't rejoin the snowball fight. She only watched. Every time Anna ducked a

snowball, she thought she saw her sister wince. It was strange—Elsa usually loved snowball fights.

Anna raced past and pelted her sister with snow. Elsa halfheartedly tossed a snowball in return. The snowball brushed Anna's head lightly, and Anna fell to the ground in mock distress. She was only joking, not hurt at all, but Elsa froze. Her face went pale with horror. She stopped playing.

"Elsa, are you all right?" Anna asked, concerned.

"I . . . I'm okay," Elsa said. But Anna could tell it wasn't true. Something was bothering her sister. "I just remembered I have to go back to the castle."

"But you don't have any appointments today!" Anna protested.

"I know. I just . . . forgot something," Elsa told her.

"We'll all go back. We'll take my sleigh," Kristoff said.

"No, really, that's okay," Elsa insisted. "You all stay and have fun. I'll walk."

Anna stared at her sister, puzzled. It wasn't like Elsa to forget anything that had to do with castle business. The only one who seemed to be forgetting was Anna.

There's something strange going on here, Anna thought. She watched as Elsa walked off alone, headed for the castle. *And I'm going to get to the bottom of it.*

Chapter 3

The next day, Anna went for a walk in the forest. Usually, she would have asked Elsa to join her. But today she felt like being alone. She wanted time to think.

Anna was still worried about her foggy childhood memories. She couldn't seem to remember anything specifically related to Elsa's magic. It was very strange. She knew Elsa had been born with her powers.

She'd had them ever since they were little. But all of Anna's memories of Elsa's magic were very recent. They took place when Elsa was queen.

Anna spent the whole morning thinking about Elsa's magic. Something about it just didn't add up. She needed to speak to Elsa directly and ask her a few questions.

Anna was on her way back to the castle when suddenly, a large rock rolled into her path. The rock tumbled end over end and came to a stop at her feet. Then it popped open! Arms and legs and a shaggy head sprang out. Anna realized it wasn't a rock at all—it was a mountain troll!

"Greetings, my lady," the troll said. He had gray skin the same color as a stone.

A tuft of grass sprouted from the top of his head between two large, round ears.

"Hello," Anna said, surprised. She'd met some of the trolls before with Kristoff, but she didn't recognize this one. She'd never seen a troll during the daytime, either.

"My name is Brock," he said with a sweeping bow. "Brock the Mystical."

"Pleased to meet you, Brock the Mystical," Anna said. "I'm—"

"I know exactly who you are, Princess Anna. Anna the Beauteous!" he exclaimed.

Anna chuckled. "My name's not Anna the Beauteous," she told him. "Just Anna."

"All right, Just Anna," Brock said. He smiled widely at her, waggling his fuzzy

eyebrows. "I think I can be of service to you, my lady."

"How?" Anna asked.

"I have many magical powers," Brock explained.

"Oh, powers," Anna said. "My sister has those. She had a little trouble with them at first."

"No trouble here, Just Anna," Brock replied.

Anna looked doubtfully at the little troll. He seemed friendly enough, but she still wondered if he might be up to something.

"Look, I should be getting back to the castle," Anna said. She stepped around Brock and started to walk away.

"Aren't you forgetting something, my lady?" Brock asked.

"I don't think so," Anna said.

"Are you sure? What about your memories?"

Anna stopped. She turned to face the troll. "What do you know about my memories?" she asked.

"If you'd like to come with me, I'll show you," he replied.

Anna thought about it, then agreed. Maybe Brock could help her solve the mystery of her missing memories. She followed him deeper into the forest.

Brock led Anna along a winding path bordered by huge trees. They walked across a small stone bridge over a babbling creek. On the bank of the creek was a wide clearing, empty of snow and dotted with piles of dried leaves and brush. In the middle stood a little thatched hut made of grasses and twigs. It had a round, wooden door not much taller than Brock himself. Anna had to duck as she followed the troll into the hut.

"Welcome to my humble home, Just Anna," Brock said.

There wasn't much in the hut. There was a small fire pit in the middle of the room. A bed made of feathers and grass sat in one corner. There were several stacks of moldy books and a few old pots and pans. Other than that, the place was bare.

"May I offer you some birchbark tea, my lady?" Brock asked, lighting a fire in the pit.

"No thanks," Anna said. She was eager to learn what Brock knew about her memories.

Once they sat down, Brock began his tale. He told Anna how the trolls were the oldest creatures in Arendelle—older than the trees! They knew all the secrets of the forest. The oldest of them, the elder troll, was a powerful healer and artist.

Anna knew an elder troll. His name was Grand Pabbie. He'd told her how to thaw a frozen heart. Grand Pabbie was very wise.

"I'll let you in on a little troll secret," Brock said. "I'm going to be just like Grand Pabbie. My powers are growing every day." He picked up a pot and held it to his ear, as if it were talking.

"Oh," Anna said, watching Brock carefully. "So what do you know about my memories?"

"Your childhood memories of magic were removed," Brock explained.

The troll went on to describe a night long ago, when little Anna and her family had traveled to the mountains to see Grand Pabbie.

Elsa had accidentally zapped her sister with a magical swirl of ice while they were playing. Their parents had rushed Anna to the trolls.

Luckily, Grand Pabbie, the troll elder, had healed Anna. But the king and queen were afraid that people would not understand Elsa's powers. To keep them a secret, Grand Pabbie removed Anna's memories of Elsa's magic. He left only her memories of having fun.

That had all been a long time ago. Elsa didn't have to hide her powers anymore.

But Anna's memories of her sister's magic were still missing!

Anna was stunned as she listened to this tale. "That's impossible," she said.

Again, she thought about growing up with Elsa. Anna remembered certain things, like catching frogs together and singing in the bathtub. But when she tried to think of anything related to magic, all she remembered was snow and laughter. Brock's story made sense.

"Not to worry, Just Anna," Brock said. "I can bring back your memories."

Anna wasn't sure. Brock seemed nice enough, but he didn't seem very wise.

Even more troubling was the thought that if Brock was right, then Elsa knew

33

what had happened. She had been there when their parents had taken Anna to Grand Pabbie. But Elsa would have told Anna about that . . . wouldn't she? Anna realized that even though they had spent a lot of time together lately, the sisters had not talked about their childhood very much.

Anna stood and bumped her head on the low ceiling of the hut. "I'm sorry," she said, rubbing her head. "But I have to go now."

Brock scrambled to his feet. "What about your memories, my lady? Surely you'll be wanting them back?"

Anna shook her head. She didn't know

what to believe. Slowly, she backed out of Brock's hut.

The troll looked disappointed, but he didn't give up. "Okay, Just Anna!" Brock called. "If you change your mind, you know where to find me!"

Chapter 4

Anna hurried toward the castle. She had a lot of questions for Elsa. If her memories of magic really had been removed, why hadn't Elsa told her?

As Anna raced across the fields not far from the castle, she passed a barn where she knew Kristoff liked to putter. Through the window, she saw that he was inside. Anna stopped running. Kristoff had grown up among the trolls. He had to know something about Brock and his story.

Anna slid open the barn door and hurried inside. Sven greeted her warmly. He nuzzled her pockets in search of carrots. Kristoff looked up from where he was polishing his sleigh.

"Don't you knock?" Kristoff asked, and then smiled.

"You're right. Where are my manners," Anna replied. She walked over to Kristoff and knocked on his sleigh.

"Hey! That's a fresh coat of lacquer!" Kristoff said.

Anna folded her arms across her chest.

"Are you ever going to actually ride in that sleigh or just polish it?" she asked.

"I ride in it all the time," he said. "That's why it needs fresh lacquer!"

Sven snorted at the two of them. The reindeer knew the only reason Anna and Kristoff pretended to argue was because they liked each other.

Anna cleared her throat. She decided to

start over. "I was hoping you could help me out," she said gently.

"Sure," Kristoff said, blushing. "What do you need help with?"

Anna told Kristoff about meeting Brock in the forest. She repeated the story the little troll had told her about the night her parents had taken her to Grand Pabbie. "So what do you think?" she asked when she was finished.

"What do I think about what?" Kristoff replied guardedly. Anna noticed that he was avoiding her gaze. He turned back to his sleigh and started polishing again.

"Is it true? About Grand Pabbie changing my memories? About Elsa not wanting to tell me?" Anna asked.

Kristoff shrugged. Anna walked around in front of him. He shifted so that he was facing away from her.

"You know something, don't you?" Anna said. She looked at him carefully.

"Who, me? Nope," Kristoff answered. Sven snorted again. Kristoff shot him a warning look. Sven snorted once more and turned away. "We know absolutely nothing."

Anna didn't believe it. She walked over to Sven.

"I know, Sven," she said. "Kristoff's hiding something."

"No, I'm not!" Kristoff responded a little too quickly.

Anna looked at Kristoff, then at Sven,

40

then back at Kristoff. Maybe there was a way for her to find out what Kristoff knew—and have a little fun while she was at it.

Anna stepped away from Sven and slid the barn door shut with a loud *THUD!* Kristoff jumped at the sound. Anna slammed the shutters closed over the windows. Suddenly, the barn was dark, except for the light of a single candle.

"Have a seat," she told Kristoff. She motioned to a chair at a small table in the corner.

Kristoff gripped his polishing rag in his fingers. He sat down at the table. Anna crossed her arms and started to pace behind him.

"True or false, you were raised by trolls?" she asked.

"Uh, true," Kristoff answered. The trolls had taken him in when he was very little. They were his family.

"True or false, you are an ice harvester?" Anna said.

"True," Kristoff replied, dropping his shoulders. He was beginning to relax.

This was all part of Anna's plan. She was going to start with the easy questions. Once Kristoff felt comfortable, she'd ask the tough ones.

"True or false," Anna said. "You know Grand Pabbie, the elder troll."

"Of course I know Grand Pabbie," Kristoff told her. At this third easy question, his face relaxed into a smile. "Grand Pabbie and I go way back."

"Since you were a little boy?" Anna continued.

Kristoff nodded.

"So you were there when Grand Pabbie changed my memories?" Anna asked casually.

"Yeah, sure I was. He just—" Kristoff stopped. "I mean—" He clapped his hands over his mouth and shook his head.

Sven snorted. "Quiet, you!" Kristoff barked.

"Let the reindeer speak!" Anna cried. Both Sven and Kristoff looked at her, puzzled. "You know what I mean!" she said. Although Anna was having fun teasing Kristoff, she also really wanted to know what he knew.

"I have ways of making you talk . . . ," she said playfully. She held up her hands as though she was going to start tickling him.

Kristoff clamped his mouth shut. He shook his head again.

Anna propped her hands on her hips. She studied her friend's face. She knew exactly how to get to him.

Anna walked over to Kristoff's sleigh. "Will you look at that?" she said to no one in particular. "What a beautiful sleigh. Is that a fresh coat of lacquer?" Anna took a measured step closer to the sleigh.

Kristoff sat up straight in his chair. His eyes grew wide.

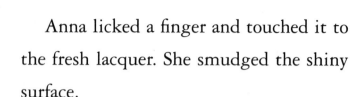

Anna licked a finger and touched it to the fresh lacquer. She smudged the shiny surface.

"Hey!" Kristoff cried. "That's my new sleigh!" He covered his eyes with his hands.

"I told you I'd make you talk!" Anna teased.

Kristoff uncovered his eyes and hung his head. After a moment, he looked up at Anna. It seemed like he was finally going to tell the truth, but then his expression changed. "Listen," he said. "It's not what you think. You should talk to your sister."

So it is true, Anna thought. Grand Pabbie had changed her memories. He'd

made it so that she couldn't remember Elsa's magic, and Elsa had known all along!

Anna's face fell. Just when she thought everything was getting back to normal, she discovered another secret.

Chapter 5

Anna wandered through the halls of the castle looking for Elsa. Part of her wanted to find her sister right away. She had so many questions! But another part of her didn't want to see Elsa at all. Everything that had happened that day just made her feel so confused.

Anna found Elsa in the Hall of Portraits. It was a long corridor filled with paintings of Arendelle's royal family. There were portraits of the former king and queen, Elsa and Anna's parents. Next to those portraits were paintings of Anna and Elsa as young girls.

Anna looked at the eight-year-old version of herself in the painting. She was smiling from ear to ear. That girl had no idea that some of her most important memories were missing.

Elsa turned and spotted Anna at the end of the hall. "There you are," Elsa said. "I was looking for you."

"I took a walk," Anna said. She turned away from Elsa as she approached.

"Anna, what's wrong?" Elsa asked, worried.

Anna hadn't been sure that she wanted to talk to Elsa. But as soon as she started to talk, it all came out.

She told her sister about her foggy memories. She told her about meeting the strange little troll in the forest. She told her the story Brock had told Anna about why her memories were missing. And she told her how it seemed that Kristoff knew what had happened.

"Did you know, too?" Anna asked.

"Anna, I'm sorry," Elsa said. Anna could see that she felt awful. "I had no choice but to hide my powers when we were little. But I have a choice now. I should have told you about Grand Pabbie's magic."

"Why didn't you?" Anna asked.

"It's just hard for me to talk about that night," Elsa said.

It hit Anna all at once. Of course Elsa didn't like to talk about the night her powers had hurt Anna. They'd almost lost each other!

"It wasn't your fault! I know you didn't mean to hurt me," Anna said, suddenly wanting to comfort her sister. She knew Elsa loved her. "But it's really strange to know that some of my past is gone. It's like a part of me is missing."

Anna hung her head. She wasn't angry with Elsa. Instead, she was sad. "I can't remember your magic, Elsa," she said glumly.

Elsa placed an arm around her sister.

"Maybe I can help you remember," she said.

"How?" Anna asked.

Elsa took Anna by the hand and led her to her room. Once inside, Elsa opened a chest at the foot of her bed. The chest held all of Elsa's keepsakes. There was a beautiful shawl given to her by their mother, her favorite childhood doll, and a special book of nursery rhymes.

Elsa set those items aside and continued to look through the chest. Next, she found a note Anna had written when she was six. The giant letters were slanted across the page. The note read *Do you wanna build a snowman?*

Elsa put the note down on the bed and
kept searching. Finally, she found what
she was looking for. At the bottom of the
chest was a small silk pouch. Elsa emptied
the pouch into the palm of her hand. Anna

gasped. There sat the most incredible piece of magical ice. There was a beautiful glass crystal frozen inside. It shimmered in the light of Elsa's room.

"Do you remember how we got this?" Elsa asked.

Anna shook her head. Elsa placed the ice crystal in Anna's hand. Then she shared her favorite memory.

Elsa would never forget the day she and Anna got their first toboggan. Their father, the King of Arendelle, had given it to them as a present.

The beautiful wooden sled had a flat

bottom. The front curved up in a delicate curl.

The king took the girls into the snowy mountains. They spent all day sledding down the steep hills. Anna and Elsa loved the toboggan so much, they wanted to keep it inside the castle with them. They even wanted the toboggan to come to dinner.

"Please!" five-year-old Anna begged her parents. "Mr. Toboggan needs to eat!"

The king and queen told the girls that the toboggan didn't need to eat. It wasn't real. It could stay outside in the carriage house with the other sleds.

Anna was disappointed, but eight-year-old Elsa knew a way to cheer her up. The next morning, before their parents woke up, Anna and Elsa crept out of bed. Elsa took Anna's hand and led her to the top of the grand staircase.

Anna rubbed her eyes sleepily. "What are we doing, Elsa?" she asked.

"Shhh! I know a way we can toboggan inside," Elsa whispered.

Anna perked up. "Is Mr. Toboggan here?" she said excitedly.

"No, but I have a better idea," Elsa replied. She closed her eyes and concentrated. A cool snow flurry rippled through the room.

Anna hugged herself to keep warm. But Elsa knew her sister didn't mind the chill. It meant Elsa was about to use her powers.

Elsa opened her eyes. She waved her

fingers through the air. Frost formed at her fingertips.

With a twirl of her hands, she created a toboggan out of pure, clear ice. The sled sparkled and glistened. Anna gasped in amazement. She hurried over to the sled and climbed in.

Elsa twirled her hands again. A huge ramp of ice formed in front of her. The ramp ran down the staircase and wound through the halls of the castle.

"That's incredible!" Anna exclaimed.

Elsa pushed the ice sled to the top of the ramp and climbed on behind Anna. "Hold on tight!" she said.

The toboggan sailed down the ramp with a *WHOOSH!* Elsa and Anna squealed with

delight. The air rushed past them, whiffling through their hair.

They tobogganed through the castle halls from one room to the next. They sped through the kitchens and barreled through the library. The icy path twisted and turned through the corridors.

As they sped along the ramp, Anna saw that it ended in a giant loop-the-loop. Her fingers gripped the front of the sled.

"Get ready!" Elsa said.

Elsa and Anna huddled together. The sled approached the loop. It flew forward, and everything was upside down! They sailed through the loop and slid to a stop.

"Woo-hoo!" Anna cried. "This is amazing!"

Elsa laughed joyfully. She'd never had so much fun!

The ice ramp ended in the castle's ballroom. The sisters scrambled from the sled. They dusted the snow off their nightgowns. Elsa looked around at the enormous dance floor. Suddenly, she had an idea.

Elsa twirled her fingers and summoned her icy powers. A magical frost settled over the floor and hardened into a smooth sheet of ice. It was the perfect surface for ice-skating, or better yet, for playing hockey! Anna dashed off to grab her ice skates and Elsa found two wooden oars to use as sticks. They returned to the ballroom and Anna laced up.

"Elsa, we forgot the puck!" Anna said.

"Not to worry," Elsa answered. She grabbed a candy dish off the mantel, used her powers to cover it in ice, and dropped it to the floor. Elsa slapped the puck with her oar. It glided across the ballroom floor with ease. Anna clapped gleefully.

"My turn! My turn!" she said.

Anna pushed off from the wall and skated after the puck. When she reached it, she drew back and took a shot at Elsa's goal, the ballroom doorway behind her. Elsa skated forward and blocked her little sister's shot. Just like that, the game had begun! The sisters skated for what seemed like hours. They were having so much fun that they lost track of time.

"ELSA! ANNA! Where are you?" cried the queen from upstairs.

Elsa stopped skating. *Uh-oh,* she thought. She put a finger to her lips, motioning for Anna to be quiet, but Anna was in midswing. She slapped the puck with all her might. It bounced off her stick with a loud *crack* and hurtled through the air. The puck stuck the ballroom's fancy chandelier, knocking loose a tiny crystal.

"Oh, no!" Anna whispered.

Elsa reached out with her powers and zapped the crystal. She sealed it in a magical piece of ice.

When it hit the ground, it didn't break. It bounced right into Elsa's hands.

Elsa held the crystal up to the light. A

rainbow of colors danced through it. Anna
stared at it in wonder.

Elsa tucked the crystal into Anna's
pocket. "It's our secret," she said, taking
Anna's hand. Anna smiled up at her big
sister.

The ramp melted quickly, along with
the sheet of ice on the ballroom floor.
Together, Elsa and Anna hurried upstairs
to meet their mother.

When Elsa finished her tale, she was
smiling from ear to ear. She looked as
happy and relaxed as Anna had ever seen

her. "I'd forgotten how much fun it is to remember," she admitted. "Thank you for reminding me."

"Thank you, Elsa," Anna said quietly. It felt as though her sister had just returned a piece of her childhood. She was eager to remember more of their time together. She was eager to remember the magic. "Is there any way you can use your powers to get my memories back?" Anna asked.

Elsa shook her head sadly. "I'm sorry, Anna, but I can't. It's not my type of magic," she explained.

Anna nodded, but she wasn't going to give up so easily. After hearing Elsa's story and seeing how happy it made her to think

about it, Anna was more determined than ever. Those memories belonged to her, too. She had to find a way to get them back for herself!

Anna closed her fingers around the ice crystal in her palm. She vowed to get her memories back, one way or another. . . .

Chapter 6

The next morning, Anna was still thinking about Elsa's story. She couldn't believe it had been erased from her memory! She remembered sledding with Elsa, and she remembered that it was fun, but that was nothing compared to the magical adventures Elsa remembered. It was an experience the sisters had shared, but only Elsa remembered the magic.

That was why Anna had come up with a plan overnight. She called it Operation Remember the Time.

The first part of Anna's plan led her to the castle library. She searched the shelves and found old family histories and journals. Anna flipped through the books, hoping they would help her remember.

There were accounts of the young princesses written by friends and relatives. There were several tales of Princess Elsa as a little girl. But there weren't any hints of her magic in the stories, other than her love of playing outside in the snow.

The ones about Anna told the story of a baby eager to walk, talk, and explore. She was always crawling off in search of adventure, and playing with her big sister.

It was wonderful to read through the family histories. Anna spent the whole morning in the library. But as afternoon approached, she was no closer to remembering.

It was time to move on to Part Two of her plan. Part Two was a return to the Hall of Portraits. Anna entered the long hallway. She stared at the paintings of her family members and ancestors. They dated back hundreds of years.

Anna walked slowly from portrait to portrait. She thought tracing her family's history might bring back some memories. She squinted and peered at the serious faces. She even recited the name of each person aloud. It was no use. Her memories of magic were still missing.

So far, Operation Remember the Time wasn't going anywhere. Anna sighed in frustration. But she wasn't done yet—she had arrived at the third and final part of her plan.

"Anna, wait!" Elsa called after her sister.

Anna marched through the halls of the castle and into the courtyard. "I have to, Elsa," she said. "If there's a chance I can get my memories back, I shouldn't waste it!"

Elsa hitched up her skirts and hurried after her sister. "But what do you really know about Brock?" she asked, concerned.

"Well, he's a troll, and trolls are magical," Anna replied.

Elsa raised an eyebrow. "That doesn't exactly sound like the best reason to trust someone."

Anna knew Elsa was probably right. Trolls were often up to mischief, and sometimes even spoke in mysterious riddles. But she had to try.

"I'm going, Elsa!" Anna said, determined. She left the courtyard and cut across the fields to the left of the castle.

"Then I'm going with you!" Elsa shouted. She ran after Anna and fell into step alongside her. Soon they walked by the barn, where Kristoff was working on his sleigh. When Kristoff saw them, he hurried outside and stood in their path.

"Hey, you!" he cried, pointing at Anna. "It took me all night to get that smudge out of the lacquer!" He cracked a smile. Kristoff was teasing her.

"Not now, Kristoff!" Anna said. She lifted her chin defiantly. "I'm on a mission."

"The last time you were on a mission, I lost my sled," Kristoff joked.

"Actually, I was hoping you could help us," Elsa said. She told Kristoff that Anna was going to Brock to get her memories back.

"Bad idea," Kristoff said. "We don't know what Brock is really up to."

"*I* do!" Anna insisted.

Kristoff looked at Anna doubtfully. "And how much did you know about Prince Hans before you trusted him?"

Anna scoffed. "That was completely different."

Elsa interrupted. "Kristoff, you lived with the trolls for a long time. Do you know anything about Brock?"

"I don't know him well," Kristoff replied. "He's not like other trolls. He lives outside the troll village in a strange hut. Before he moved out on his own, his attempts at mystical powers always caused accidents. The trolls call him Brock the Rock, because he's about as smart as a rock."

"I saw him during the day!" Anna

offered. "Trolls are usually only seen at night. Maybe that means he really is mystical."

"Or maybe it just means he's strange," Kristoff replied.

"Hmm, maybe he's not the best choice," Elsa said gently. "Could we go to see Grand Pabbie?"

Kristoff shook his head. "Grand Pabbie's hibernating for a while," he said. "He'll be back when the seasons turn."

"I'm not waiting till the seasons turn!" Anna said. "I'm giving Brock a chance!"

"Then it's settled." Elsa gave a nod. "We're going to see Brock, and Kristoff is coming with us. Don't make me *command* it," she added with a smile.

Anna smiled, too. As the Queen of Arendelle, Elsa had a way of getting what she wanted. Anna was glad that today, what Elsa wanted was to help her sister, even if it was a long shot. The three friends set off into the forest.

Chapter 7

It was several hours before Anna found the familiar trail through the forest. She, Elsa, and Kristoff followed the path. They crossed the stone bridge over the babbling creek. At last, they came to Brock's grassy hut.

Anna knocked on the round wooden door. The three visitors heard shuffling inside. Moments later, the door flew open. Brock's shaggy head popped out.

"Just Anna! It's you! And you've brought friends!" Brock cried excitedly. He stood back and waved them into his home.

Anna, Elsa, and Kristoff ducked through the small round door. Elsa and Anna sat down beside the fire pit in the center of the hut. Brock sat across from them. There wasn't enough room near the fire for Kristoff. He wedged himself into a corner and sat down on a pile of moldy books.

"No, no!" Brock said. "Do not crush the books! Books are our friends!"

Kristoff frowned. He stood with his head ducked and his shoulders hunched.

Anna introduced everyone to Brock. The troll recognized Elsa. "Brock the Mystical, my queen," he said, and gallantly kissed her hand. He also knew of Kristoff, the man-child raised by trolls.

"Dreadful manners," Brock said, staring at Kristoff.

"I'll say," Anna agreed with a grin. Kristoff smirked at her.

Changing the subject, Anna told Brock that she had come to take him up on his offer. She wanted her memories of Elsa's magic back. Now that everyone knew about Elsa's powers, there was no reason for Grand Pabbie's spell to stay in place. It was time for her to remember.

"I was hoping you'd change your mind, my lady," Brock said. He clapped his hands delightedly. He looked confident and eager to get to work.

Maybe this will actually work, Anna thought.

To restore Anna's memories, Brock said, he had to brew a special potion.

Kristoff's frown deepened. "Grand Pabbie never brews potions," he said. The elder troll's powers came from within. Potions had nothing to do with them.

Elsa noticed Kristoff's frown and gave him a warning glance. Kristoff grumbled but said nothing more.

Brock sent his three visitors into the forest to gather special plants. The plants would make up the ingredients for his potion. Elsa, Anna, and Kristoff split up to find the ingredients.

Anna made her way through the woods. She was looking for a plant called Wyrm's Tail. Brock had told her that it grew in dark places, like underneath rocks.

Anna picked up the rocks and stones

along her path. Eventually, she found one with a plant growing under it. The plant had long, spindly branches that looked like worms. She carefully pulled it out of the dark soil, roots and all.

On her way back to Brock's hut, she met Elsa. Elsa carried a handkerchief full of fresh herbs.

"Do you really think this will work, Anna?" Elsa asked.

Anna thought for a moment. "I hope it will," she said. "It's important for me to have my memories, Elsa. *All* of my memories."

"Then I hope it works, too," Elsa said.

Back at Brock's hut, a fire blazed under a bubbling cauldron. The ingredients had all been gathered. Brock tossed them into the pot. He stirred them together. The little troll beamed happily as his potion brewed.

Steam rose from the cauldron. Anna, Elsa, and Kristoff wrinkled their noses. The smell was awful.

"How do you think the potion works?" Anna whispered to Elsa.

"I'm not sure," Elsa answered. "But I have a feeling you'll have to drink it."

"All of these herbs are safe to eat," Kristoff chimed in. "But I wouldn't want to taste it."

Ten minutes later, the potion was ready. Anna's worst fears were confirmed. Brock dipped a cup into the smelly brown brew. He handed it to Anna.

"Drink, my lady," Brock said. "It's a memory draught. It will help restore your past."

Anna pinched her nose with her fingers. She closed her eyes and quickly gulped the potion down.

"Yuck!" she exclaimed.

"Splendid!" Brock said. He circled the cauldron three times on his stocky legs. All the while, he chanted in a mysterious language. Brock said that it was the secret language of the trolls.

"I didn't know the trolls had a secret language," Anna whispered.

"They don't!" Kristoff scoffed from his place in the corner.

"Silence, Book Crusher!" Brock said.

Kristoff clamped his mouth shut. He folded his arms across his chest and rolled his eyes.

Brock turned his attention back to Anna. He explained that she, too, would have to circle the cauldron. Anna stood and started to walk, but Brock interrupted her.

"Ah, I should have been more specific," he said. "You'll have to hop around the pot on one foot."

Anna hopped awkwardly around the cauldron. Kristoff grinned at her from the corner. She knew she must look absolutely ridiculous. Anna scowled at Kristoff, but she kept hopping.

"Very good," Brock said when Anna

was done. "Now cluck like a chicken."

Anna exchanged a doubtful glance with her sister. Was Brock serious?

Elsa shrugged. "Sometimes there's no explaining magic," she whispered.

Reluctantly, Anna clucked. She clucked for at least five minutes. Finally, Brock told her it was okay to stop. When she did, the hut was silent, except for Kristoff snickering in the background.

Anna glared at him, but she didn't have time to stay angry.

"The magic is complete!" Brock announced. "It's time to test your memories, Just Anna."

Chapter 8

Anna looked at Brock, puzzled. She didn't feel much different than she had a few minutes earlier. Her stomach was queasy from the awful potion, but she didn't think that was because of magic. It seemed impossible that hopping and clucking could bring her memories back.

Anna thought about the way Elsa's magic worked. She didn't have to hop about or make strange noises. It wasn't silly. If anything, it was beautiful. Elsa could make snow appear. She could build castles of ice with a twirl of her fingers. She didn't need a cauldron.

But Anna was still hopeful. Just because Brock's magic looked different didn't mean it didn't work.

"Now I'm going to ask you some questions, Just Anna," Brock said. "The answers will prove that my magic has worked!"

Anna nodded. Elsa looked at Brock expectantly.

"First question: what color is the sky?" Brock asked.

"Blue," Anna answered.

The troll looked very pleased. "What color is your hair?" he asked.

"Red," Anna replied easily.

"What does this have to do with anything?" Kristoff grumbled.

"I beg you not to interrupt, Book Crusher," Brock said. Kristoff opened his mouth to argue, but Elsa silenced him with a look.

Brock looked eagerly at Anna. "What is your favorite food?"

"Chocolate," Anna said.

"Aha!" Brock exclaimed. "Success! Your memory is saved, Just Anna!"

"Brock, you offered to restore my memories of Elsa's magic! From our

childhood! None of those questions had anything to do with magic!" Anna said.

Brock the Mystical scratched his chin thoughtfully. "Oh, right," he said. "I knew I forgot something. Maybe you should cluck some more."

Anna's mind clouded with disappointment. Brock wasn't mystical. He certainly wasn't going to be powerful like Grand Pabbie. He was nothing more than a kooky little troll who liked to brew awful potions.

Anna's shoulders slumped. She glanced at Elsa and Kristoff, expecting them to say "I told you so." But they both looked just as disappointed as she felt. Anna realized suddenly that they both had been hoping it would work, too. They really cared about her. It made Anna feel just a little bit better.

"Listen, Anna, maybe you should try to remember something about *us,*" Elsa said quietly.

"Like what?" Anna asked sadly.

"Like anything," Elsa replied. "Like that time we went ice fishing by ourselves on the frozen lake."

Anna's face brightened. She remembered that story like it was yesterday. Eagerly, she shared it with Kristoff, Brock, and Elsa.

℮lsa and Anna's mother, the Queen of
Arendelle, used to take her daughters ice
fishing. The queen had loved to fish with
her family since she was a little girl. She
was good at it, too. She was proud to pass
on the tradition to her daughters.

In the winter, the queen would take the
princesses to the frozen lake. She taught
them how to build a shelter on the ice. Once
inside the shelter, the queen carved a hole
in the ice. She showed Elsa and Anna how
to bait their hooks and cast their fishing
lines. They would sit all day with their

lines lowered through the hole. They kept warm in their shelter, waiting for the fish to bite.

One day, the girls asked their father to take them ice fishing. The queen was away visiting relatives. He promised to take Elsa and Anna the next day, but the sisters just couldn't wait.

Eight-year-old Elsa and five-year-old Anna grabbed their fishing lines. They bundled up in their warmest coats. When no one was looking, they sneaked out of the castle.

Back in the present, Kristoff interrupted Anna's story with a question. "You two made it all the way from the castle to the frozen lake by yourselves?" he asked.

Anna considered his question. Her brow furrowed in thought. "I guess we did," she said uncertainly. The more she thought about it, all she could remember was snow and laughter.

"Actually, we didn't. We had help," Elsa said.

Anna noticed the glimmer of mischief in her sister's eyes. "You used your powers," she said.

Elsa nodded. She explained that she'd built a magical sailboat out of ice. The

94

sails were spun from a delicate web of snowflakes. The winter wind blew and filled the snowflake sails, carrying the sisters all the way to the frozen lake.

Anna shared more of the story. Once they'd arrived at the lake, they built a shelter, just like their mother had taught them.

"Well, not *just like* she taught us," Elsa said.

Anna glanced at her sister again. Elsa admitted that she'd used her powers then, too. She'd built them a miniature castle on the ice.

Anna remembered that they'd stayed out all afternoon and caught a lot of fish.

Elsa chimed in to add the magical details. The ice boat had carried them home with their baskets of fish. Elsa froze the fish and snuck them into the kitchens.

"Fishsicles!" five-year-old Anna had shouted in delight.

Afterward, the royal family had eaten fish for weeks. The king and queen never knew exactly why there was so much fish at the dinner table.

"This is wonderful!" Brock said when the story was over. "My magic saved the day!" Before they could pull away, the troll spread his arms wide and squeezed Anna, Elsa, and Kristoff together in an awkward hug. Unfortunately, he accidentally kicked

a burning coal from beneath the pot.

The coal leaped across the room. It landed next to the pile of moldy books in the corner. Seconds later, one of the books caught fire!

"What's that smell?" Anna asked.

Kristoff broke free of Brock's group hug. He spotted the burning book in the corner of the hut. "Fire!" he yelled. Immediately, Kristoff raised his foot to stomp out the flames.

Brock wailed unhappily. "Stop, Book Crusher! Don't crush my books!" The troll dove across the hut and grabbed the flaming book. He juggled it in his hands like a hot potato.

"What are you doing?" Kristoff shouted angrily.

"Saving a friend!" Brock cried. He tossed the book out of the hut, beyond Kristoff's reach.

The book sailed through the air. It landed in a patch of dry bushes and quickly sent them up in flames. Anna, Elsa, Kristoff, and Brock raced outside. What they saw wasn't pretty. The forest was catching fire!

Chapter 9

Brock the Rock looked on in horror. The fire was spreading rapidly. It leaped from bush to bush. Some of the trees were even starting to catch—Anna hadn't noticed until that moment that most of the tall trees around Brock's clearing were dead and dry, their brown leaves dangling from their branches. The orange flames crackled and hissed.

Burning leaves tumbled from the trees. The leaves landed on the roof of Brock's grass cottage. Within seconds, the roof caught fire.

"Oh, no!" Brock shouted. He waved his arms frantically. The kooky troll had no idea what to do. He puckered his lips and blew at the flames, hoping to put them out.

"Stop!" Kristoff cried. "This is a forest fire, not a birthday cake! You can't just blow it out!"

Kristoff leaped into action. He heaved his shoulder against the side of the burning grass hut. Anna saw what he was trying to do. She and Elsa pushed against

the sides of Brock's house and knocked it to the ground.

Once the flimsy grass house had fallen, Anna, Elsa, and Kristoff stomped out the flames.

"I'm sorry, Brock," Anna said.

Anna heard a branch crack and looked up at the trees surrounding the clearing. The flames were spreading even farther than she'd thought. She saw her sister gazing at the fire and caught her eye. She could tell Elsa was about to use her magic. She gave her a questioning look.

"It's too big," Elsa said. "I'm not sure I can do it alone."

Brock looked sadly at what was left of

his home. Elsa placed a gentle hand on his shoulder. "We'll build you a new house, Brock, I promise. But right now we have to stop this fire!"

"That's right," Anna said to the troll. "Just think, what would Grand Pabbie do?"

At the mention of Grand Pabbie, Brock's face brightened. "Grand Pabbie would help put out the fire!"

"We need buckets!" Kristoff called, watching the flames. "Anything we can use to carry water."

"I have an idea, Just Anna!" Brock said.

He poked through the smoldering grass of his house. After a moment, he pulled out the large cauldron, along with

several cooking pots. "Will these do?" he asked.

"Brock, they're perfect!" Anna said. She picked up the cauldron and handed the pots to Kristoff. Brock found some old buckets and raced to the nearby brook.

Anna, Kristoff, and Brock filled their pots with water while Elsa sprayed the trees with ice. Anna paused to watch her sister. It seemed that for every tree she put out, two more caught fire.

The others lugged the water back to Brock's house and tossed it on the burning trees. The fire kept spreading. The flames were growing higher and higher.

Kristoff realized that they couldn't

carry enough water to put out the flames. "We need help!" he said.

Anna volunteered to run to the valley and gather more trolls to help fight the fire. She hurried through the forest to where she remembered meeting the trolls before. Anna rounded up as many as she could. They were eager to help. They followed Anna through the woods.

By the time Anna returned, the clearing where Brock's house had been was engulfed in flames. Elsa, Kristoff, and Brock had fallen back deeper into the forest.

Anna organized the volunteers. She had them form a chain from the brook to the clearing. She stood in the stream, filling

pots with water. They passed the pots down the line of trolls. At the opposite end of the line, Kristoff and Brock were waiting. They tossed pot after pot of water on the fire.

The fire sizzled and hissed. Smoke rose high into the air. Finally, the flames in the clearing began to die down. But by then it was too late. The fire had spread too far. Flames darted across the treetops. A cloud of thick smoke hung over the woods.

Elsa was trying to control the spreading by putting out the fire one tree at a time. "This isn't working fast enough!" Anna heard her sister call out. "I need to see which way it's going!"

Just then, Anna saw something large rising out of the forest. Elsa was using her magic to form a tall column of ice under her feet. Now she would be able to see the entire fire. Elsa raised her arms toward the sky and closed her eyes, deep in concentration.

A cold wind began to blow. It rustled through the leaves. The trolls stopped passing pots. They looked at Elsa.

Elsa opened her eyes. She weaved her hands through the air. A thick blanket of snow drifted down from the clouds above the forest.

The snow fell heavily onto the flames. The fire hissed and sputtered, but it was

no match for Elsa's powers. The magical snowflakes simply outnumbered the embers. Soon the sparks were smothered. The flames had died out at last.

Chapter 10

After the smoke cleared, the trolls gave a hearty cheer. They were relieved that Queen Elsa had stopped the fire and that no one had been hurt. The forest was safe once again.

The trolls invited Brock to stay with them until his hut was rebuilt. Anna, Elsa, and Kristoff helped him gather his belongings from the rubble. The damage wasn't as bad as they had first thought. They were even able to save some of his moldy books.

Brock was still convinced that his potion had restored Anna's memories. Kristoff was eager to tell him the truth, but Anna didn't have the heart. Brock had tried his best to help her. The troll deserved to remember as much magic as he wanted to.

That night at the castle, Anna and Elsa sat down to dinner. Anna was excited to recall the day's events.

"I can't believe I actually clucked like a chicken!" she said.

"I can't believe you actually drank that

awful potion," Elsa laughed. "The smell was horrible!"

Anna thought about how determined she had been to get her memories back. It had been important to her to remember on her own. Only that morning, she had felt like a puzzle with pieces missing. But this afternoon, all that had changed.

Anna realized that her memories weren't missing. As long as Elsa was there, the puzzle was complete. Elsa could remember the magic and Anna could remember the laughter. Together, they were a winning combination.

Elsa looked at Anna across the

dinner table. She must have noticed the thoughtful expression on her sister's face. "I'm sorry I didn't tell you sooner about your memories, Anna," she said. "But I'll always be here for you. We can help each other remember."

Anna nodded. She got up from the table, walked over to Elsa, and hugged

her sister tight. "I have just one question for you," she said. "How come I can't remember all the times we built snowmen together?"

Anna still found that very strange. She had only bits and pieces of those memories. She remembered finding buttons to use for eyes. She remembered sneaking carrots from the kitchens to use as noses. She even remembered gathering hats and scarves for the snowmen to wear. But she could never remember building an actual snowman with Elsa.

"Snowmen were your favorite, Anna," Elsa said. "You were always asking me to make them."

Anna always said that her sister built the best snowmen. Elsa knew how to make special snowman snow—fluffy enough to carry but wet enough to pack into the perfect snowball. Elsa's snowmen always seemed so real. It was easy to imagine their button eyes winking in the light and their carrot noses twitching in the crisp winter air.

On the morning of Anna's fifth birthday, she woke up to a soft sprinkle of snowflakes above her bed. They drifted down from the ceiling of her room. But these weren't

just any snowflakes. Each one was like a tiny sculpture made of ice crystals. One snowflake looked just like Anna! Another looked like Elsa! There were reindeer snowflakes and snowflakes of the king and queen. Best of all, there were snowman snowflakes!

Anna was delighted. She noticed that the snowflakes were falling in a clear path leading out of her room. Eagerly, she hopped out of bed and followed the snowflake path through the castle.

The path led downstairs and out the front door. Anna pulled on a warm coat and followed the trail outside to the royal sleigh.

In the sleigh, Elsa was waiting.

"Happy birthday, Anna!" she told her sister.

Anna giggled happily.

A team of reindeer pulled the sleigh. They drove the sisters all the way to the frozen fjord. There, Elsa gave Anna her birthday present. It was a brand-new pair of ice skates!

Elsa helped Anna lace up her skates. The sisters stepped out onto the fjord. They glided easily across the ice.

Anna and Elsa skated together all afternoon. They whirled and twirled and carved pictures into the ice. Elsa even carved a beautiful picture of Anna wearing a birthday crown.

As evening fell, the girls stopped skating. It was time to build a special snowman for Anna's birthday. Elsa swirled her fingers through the air. She created a mound of her famous snowman snow.

Together, Anna and Elsa rolled the snow into three giant snowballs. Elsa stacked them on top of each other. Anna was excited. She wanted to stick on the button eyes and carrot nose, but she was too short. Elsa created a small set of ice steps for her sister. Anna climbed the steps and made the snowman's face.

That night, Elsa led a sleepy Anna to bed. She tucked her little sister in and said good night. Anna drifted off to sleep.

The next morning, Anna ran to Elsa's bedroom and shared her dream. In it, she'd sung and danced with an enchanted snowman. She asked Elsa if she could use her powers to make their snowman dance. Elsa smiled. She told Anna that she couldn't make a dancing snowman, but they could always pretend. Together, they could imagine anything.

Back in the present, Elsa finished sharing the memory. Anna felt another piece of her past slide into place. Hearing Elsa tell the story was almost like being there.

"It's funny, Elsa," Anna said. "I was so worried about not being able to remember your magic, I forgot about the magic right here."

"What do you mean?" Elsa asked.

"This. Us," Anna replied. "There's magic in remembering together."

"There sure is," Elsa said. She smiled.

She and Anna walked out of the dining room. They'd had a long day fighting a forest fire and remembering the past. Soon it would be time to go to bed. As they walked up the grand staircase to their rooms, Anna turned to her sister.

"You know, Elsa, snowmen aren't my favorite anymore," she said.

"Really?" Elsa asked. "You seem pretty fond of Olaf."

"Oh, yes, I love Olaf, but he's not my favorite," Anna replied. "You are."